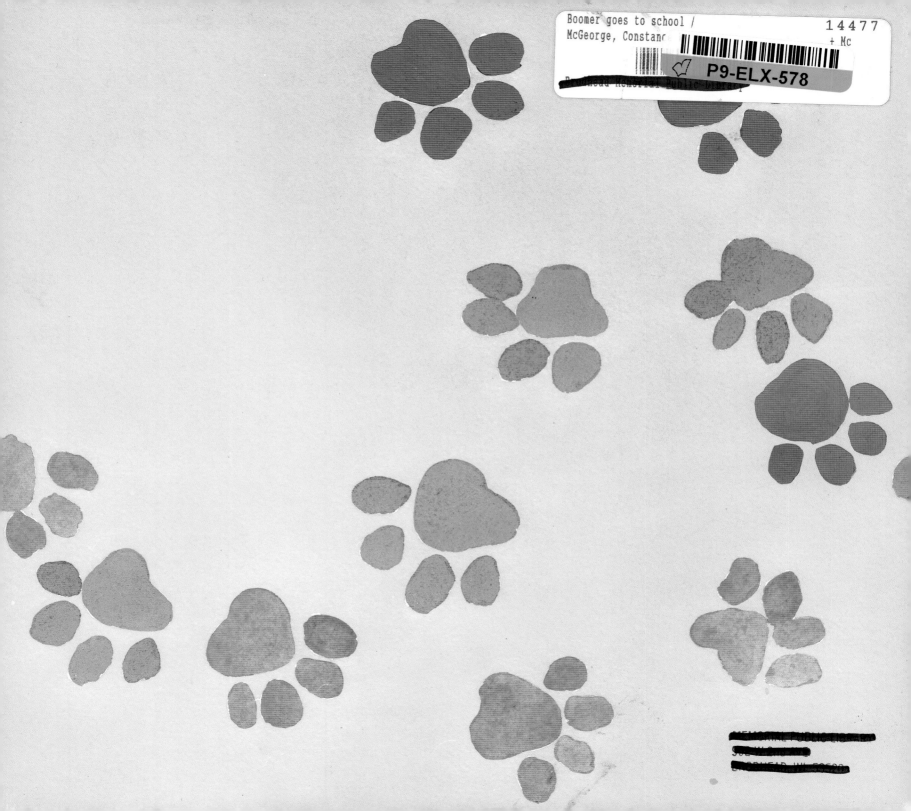

With love for my sister Ginny —C.W.M.

With love for Charles and Thomas —M.W.

With love for the 3 R's—
Running, Retrieving, and Recess —BOOMER

Text © 1996 by Constance W. McGeorge

Illustrations © 1996 Mary Whyte

All rights reserved.

Book design by Suellen Ehnebuske/Lucy Nielsen.

Typeset in Syntax and Providance Sans.

Printed in Hong Kong.

Library of Congress Cataloging in Publication Data.

McGeorge, Constance W.

Boomer goes to school/

by Constance W. McGeorge: illustrated by Mary Whyte

Summary: Boomer, the golden retriever, accompanies

his owner to school for show and tell.

ISBN: 0-8118-1117-4 (HC)

[1. Golden retreivers—Fiction. 2. Dogs—Fiction.

3. School—Fiction.] I. Whyte, Mary, ill. II. Title

PZ7.M478467B1   1996   95-38278

[E]—dc20   CIP

                                 AC

Distributed in Canada by Raincoast Books

8680 Cambie Street

Vancouver B.C. V6P 6M9

Chronicle Books

85 Second Street

San Francisco, California 94105

Website: www.chronbooks.com

10   9   8   7   6   5   4   3

Boomer Goes to School

By Constance W. McGeorge

Illustrated by Mary Whyte

CHRONICLE BOOKS • SAN FRANCISCO

Boomer was just settling down after his morning walk, when suddenly, someone called his name. Then, Boomer saw his leash.

Boomer was very excited—he thought he was going for another walk.

But instead, Boomer and his owner raced outside,
down the driveway, and onto a big yellow bus.
Boomer was going for a ride!

The bus stopped again and again. Boomer had
never been on a ride with so many children.
The ride was very noisy.

After a while, the bus stopped in front of a big building.
The children climbed out. Boomer climbed out, too.
He was quickly led inside, up some stairs, around a
corner, and down a hallway.

Finally, Boomer's owner stopped at an open door.

Boomer looked in. It was a room filled with desks, tables, chairs, and children.

As Boomer was led to the back of the room, a loud bell rang. A grownup started talking. Everyone sat down and listened.

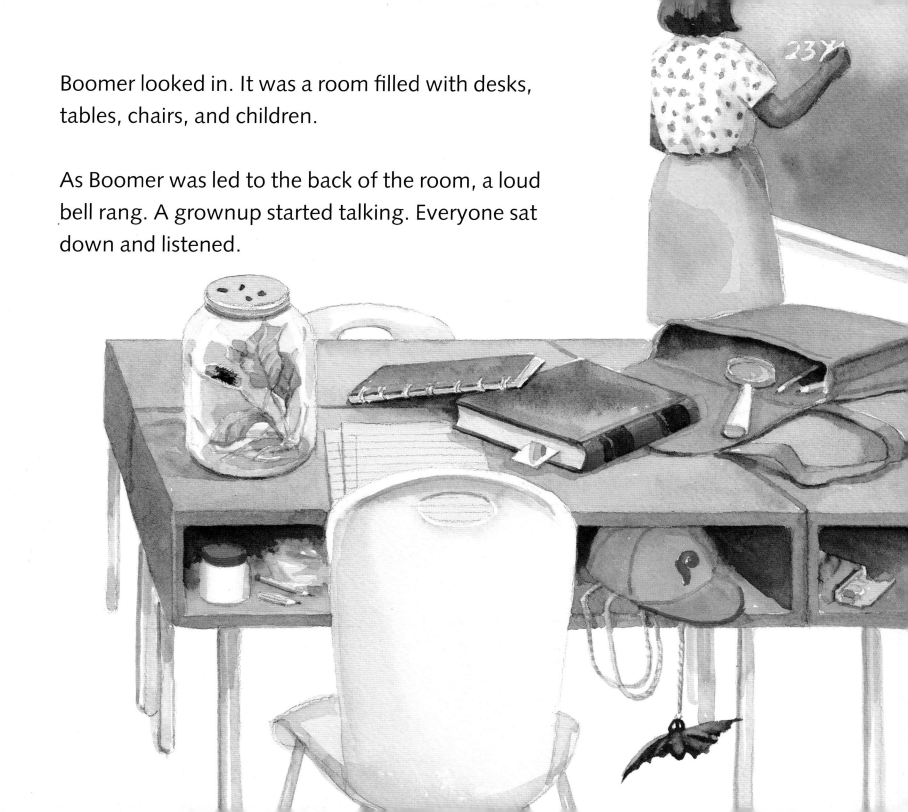

When the grownup finished talking, the children jumped up from their seats. Boomer was let off his leash. He didn't know what to do first!

There were toys to share . . .

. . . pictures to paint . . .

. . . games to play . . .

and best of all . . . there was lunch!

After lunch, Boomer watched as the children gathered together and sat in a circle. Boomer was ready for the next game. But this time, all the children sat quietly.

Boomer started to get up, but he was told to sit down.

Boomer wiggled and squirmed. He was told to sit still.

Boomer barked and barked.
He was told to be quiet.

Boomer was very confused.

Then, Boomer was led to the center of the circle. He still wiggled and squirmed. Boomer's owner started talking—sharing stories about Boomer and showing him to the class.

Finally, Boomer understood. He sat still and stayed very quiet. Boomer's owner smiled and gave Boomer a big pat on the head!

Suddenly, a loud bell rang and it was time to take another bus ride. At each bus stop, Boomer's new friends patted him good-bye.

Then, the bus stopped at Boomer's house. Boomer wagged his tail and bounded off the bus for home.

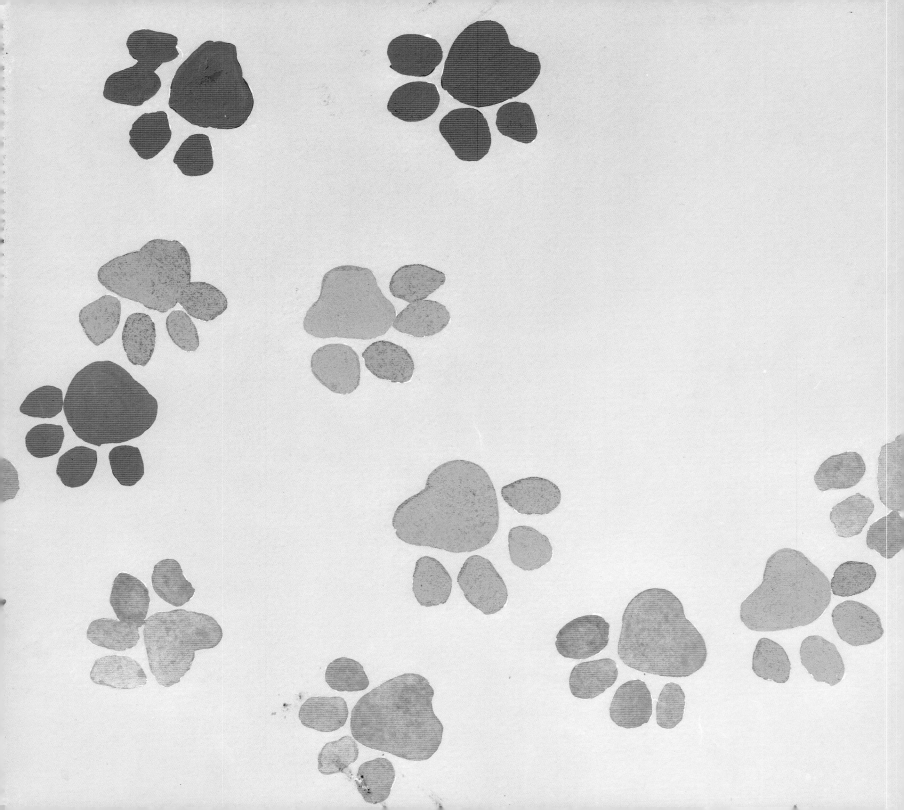